I0630902

Bad Boy Billionaire

J.L. Ryan

Published by J.L. Ryan, 2018.

BAD BOY BILLIONAIRE

First edition. June 1, 2018.

Copyright © 2018 J.L. Ryan.

ISBN: 978-1393999010

Written by J.L. Ryan.

The Bad Boy's Secret

Frantic with worry, Amelia Randolph was fuming. Her grandmother was sick again, and it had to be the water. She paced the room in the hospital where she watched her grandmother sleeping. Nothing had been right in a long time, not since that arrogant billionaire, Jacob Montgomery had his company install a new water filtration system in her home.

She'd had her suspicions for a long time, but then they tested it, and she knew she had to be right. Toxic chemicals were found in the water supply. She called, prodded, and attacked everyone she could in order to get answers. It wasn't that she couldn't be a lady, she could. Her grandmother was the most important person to her and there was no way she could just stand idly by and wait for things to get worse.

Friday, she would get her chance, until then, she was doing her best to keep calm. If she went too crazy beforehand, she may not be able to state her case, and she had to. She looked over at the woman nestled into the bed that seemed to swallow her up in its massive size

"I'll, fix it Nana, I will." She whispered the words to herself. Her grandmother had been asleep for an hour now and a sounder sleeper you would never meet.

She caught a glimpse of herself in the mirror near the doorway. Her normally tamed head of hair was a jumbled mess. She was an average girl, at least she thought so. At 5'7 she was taller than many girls, she had dark green eyes and was in pretty good shape. She wasn't perfect by any means. She filled out her clothes nicely and was curvy. She was far from the model stick thin types most men preferred. Her hair was naturally curly and hung down past her shoulders.

There must have been 4 different shades of red mixed in there. Today what she needed most was some conditioner and a pony tail. She glanced over at the table where lunch had been placed and noticed a rubber band, it would have to do. With a shrug, she wrapped her hair in a severe bun and at least managed to contain the wild mess.

She took a seat by the large window in the room and opened a book. Reading calmed her and had always been a favorite pastime. There was something magical about being swept away into someone else's fantasy world. It made thing easier, especially when times got dark. She gave her Nana another look over. She had saved her life, literally. She owed her everything, and wouldn't stop short of giving her as much back. She would fix this mess, or die trying.

It had been twelve years since her life had changed for the better. At 26 there wasn't a day that went by that she didn't remember, and take time to appreciate the life she had now. Her mother had been an angry, bitter woman. That's pretty much all she could remember about her. She'd had Amelia young, they could have been sisters really. Her life had been hard and full of everything negative. Amelia could remember being hungry, and cold more often than not.

Her mother was always entertaining one man or another. Whatever money she made prostituting she would spend on drugs, throwing her son and daughter a crumb or two from time to time. When Amelia turned 10, things got even worse.

She felt the sadness well up in her, even now. Her brother's name was Evan. He was always a sweet boy, and often sick. He was younger by five years and Amelia tried her best to protect him. He never hurt anyone in his whole life and he could have been something wonderful. The day he disappeared was the longest day of her life.

Her mother was running late as always, and they were starving. She was only 10 years old, and she knew they could go to the neighbor's house and Miss Sinclair would help them. She was always giving them bread and candies. She had specifically told Evan to stay at the house. She had tucked him into the cot in their corner of the room and told him to wait and she would get them some food.

He had smiled up at her and she hugged him before going. It was the last time she would ever see him. Miss Sinclair wasn't home, but on her way back to their house someone had seen her, had followed her. He was a big man, he smelled of whiskey and smoke.

He grabbed her by the arm and refused to let go despite her kicking and screaming. With a kick to the groin, she had finally broken free and she ran, probably faster than she ever would again in her life. She made it home, and Evan was gone. She frantically looked for him, but there was no sign of him.

When her mother made it home finally she told her, but was ignored. Her mother just told her he was probably off playing somewhere. She felt helpless and lost, and she never wanted to feel like that again. Her thoughts were always with Evan, even now. Not long after the county had come and taken her away. She couldn't save him, but she could do something about her Nana.

There was something special in the air the day Lenora Randolph came to Bakerstown Girls Home. It may have been because her birthday was the day before or it may have been the way it was supposed to snow that week, which rarely happened in South Carolina. Whatever it was, you could almost feel it. Amelia had lived there for 2 years, and in her mind it was wonderful.

She had her very own bed and clothes and they always had food. When the people had put her here she had been scared, but over time she realized that it was wonderful. She didn't sleep at night for a long time, but gradually she had stopped having nightmares and now she felt more like everyone else.

There were always people coming there, looking to adopt a girl to love as their very own, but she never thought much about it. Babies and young girls were always the ones chosen. That was something she has been just fine with. Out there you never know who will come around, who will hurt you. Here she was safe. She knew everyone who worked there and she also knew they locked the doors every night. Inside the girls home, she didn't have to worry. It was a shock to her when a nice lady had come around to greet all of the older girls in her wing.

It was a rare occurrence and while everyone was putting on their best clothes she just went about her normal routine. Eventually the lady had asked her what her name was and the conversation they had that day changed her life forever.

"What is your name young lady?" The lady smiled at her as she sat down on the bed beside her.

"Me? My name is Amelia. How do you do?" she had thrust her hand out like she saw them do on television and the lady shook it in return.

"How are you doing today? I hear there is snow in the forecast." The lady had leaned over and smiled at her as they talked. Amelia smiled back, she was nice and she smelled like cookies.

"I'm okay. I guess. Sure, is getting colder that's for sure, but I like it. I used to hate it when I lived out there and I didn't have heat, boy it was no fun at all. Now I hope to get to see some snow real soon." She went back to making her bed.

"It sounds like you have done a lot of stuff in your life, Amelia."

"I guess so, you see how everyone is running around and trying so hard to be their best? I just don't understand that at all. I just want to be me all the time, so I don't make anyone sad when they find out who I really am. That's why I ain't dressed up in the Sunday clothes. I hate to be a pest Ma'am, but could you stand up? I just have to get this bed made so I can get to breakfast. I am always hungry and I sure like to eat."

Amelia had given her a grin as the lady had jumped up quickly. She made her bed and gave the lady a hug before she headed down to the lunch hall.

"You sure smell nice, lady." Amelia skipped her way out of the room and thought nothing more of the situation, and the lady she had left upstairs.

Later that day the nice lady had asked her if she wanted to come live with her and at first, she had said no. The lady had sat back on the chair in the library and watched Amelia for a moment before asking her why.

"It's not you lady, you seem real nice, honest. The thing is, there are a lot of bad people out there. Here they lock up the doors real tight and it's safe that's all. I guess, I just don't know how you do things. I don't want to get hurt like I did before. I don't want them to take me like they did Evan."

"Who is Evan, dear?"

She had leaned over and whispered. "I'm not supposed to talk about Evan. No one believes me about him. He was my brother and one day someone took him."

The lady had frowned for a second and told her. "Amelia, I can assure you one thing. I lock my house up every night, just like they do here. I am all alone in there and sometimes I want someone to talk to. I had a nice man who I was married to his name was Harold but he died and he is in Heaven now. I can't promise you won't ever get hurt again, the world is full of hurt, but I can promise I'll be there with you to help you through it."

She had frowned as she thought over what the cookie lady had said. She had locks, and she was sad too. Plus, she would have someone to help her and it was nice to hear someone say that. She would miss her friends here, but maybe she should go, the lady seemed real sad and maybe she could help her.

She smiled her best smile and agreed to go. She gathered up her small bag of things and with a deep breath she had walked out of the children's home and into the arms of her loving Nana. Her life had changed for the better, and Nana was the reason. She owed her so much and it was killing her to see her sick like this. Everything that she had gone through Nana had made it better, even if it was just a hug when the boy at school was mean to her or helping her by sitting with her through a panic attack.

Even now she still had those, when she couldn't be in control. Either way, her Nana fixed everything for her, she would do the same for her now. She glanced up at the clock in the room and sighed. She needed to work, that always helped keep her mind occupied. After another glance at her Nana she left to get some work done.

Jacob Montgomery worked hard and he deserved the nicer things in life. He wasn't cocky or overly confident. He didn't think he was some gorgeous Brad Pitt all women wanted. He did, however, think he was a good man, and he tried hard to do the right thing. It was the reason the mess he was in was so difficult.

He looked down at the picture in his hand and sighed. Amelia Randolph was becoming a problem he didn't want or need. He put the picture of the plant back down and raked his hand through his dark hair. Ever since the water had tested positive for some abnormal chemical content she had been blowing up his office day and night.

It wasn't that he didn't care, in fact, he was just as concerned as she was. The problem was she was a screeching, loud, demanding woman and he wasn't relishing the idea of having a meeting with her at all. There were steps that had to take place and he was only part of the board.

For whatever reason, she felt like somehow, it was all his fault. He had tried to call her back, only to get her voicemail, which in turn, had led to the meeting they were having on Friday morning. He wanted to give her the good news, for her grandmother's well-being, and to get her to stop leaving long winded, potty mouthed voice mails on his phone at work. He glanced out the long window in his office. It had been a long and windy road to get to this place.

At age 31 he had achieved more success than any other Montgomery before him. His great-grandfather had started this business and since then it had grown leaps and bounds. It had passed down to each Montgomery until now it rested on him. He could remember as a child watching his father, work the phones, spend his evening planning and most importantly dress sharp.

There was something about a great suit that made a man. Having something tailored to you was one of the luxuries he enjoyed as the CEO. He didn't drink, or do drugs and he worked effortlessly putting in long hours to make the business a success, and well, he liked nice suits. It gave him that extra push to do well and added to the confidence of representing the company well. It had started with his grandfather and one day he would pass this entire empire down to his children. That is, If he ever got married.

Jessalyn crossed his mind and he smiled. She was a wildcat if there ever was one. The wealthy daughter of a fashion designer they crossed paths on occasion and he had been taken in right away. She was a leggy blonde, her features almost too perfect, most likely due to a random number of surgeries. Despite the insincerity of her looks he liked her inquisitive nature and they had enjoyed each other's company for the last two years.

More often than not he would call ahead when he would be in town and she would make time for him, and vice versa. She was often away for modeling shoots and he was away for some business deal or another. On the rare occasion that their calendars would sync up they would get together and try to be "normal." She knew his world, the demands of it and never complained.

They never took things any deeper than a mutual respect and a great sex life. The last time he had seen her had been three months ago, and everything had changed. Somewhere along the way she had fallen in love with a model named Brutus and she couldn't meet for a rendezvous anymore.

He tried to gauge his feelings on it. He was stuck somewhere between relieved and lonely. He didn't have time for anything serious, and yet he hated never having anyone to spend time with. One of the benefits of that was that he had more time to focus on the task at hand, the water treatment system his company had installed a few towns over that could be making people sick. That brought his thoughts back to

Miss Randolph and he cringed. It was going to be a long week, and an even longer Friday.

The weather in South Carolina has been never predictable. The winters would range from snow and ice to a mild 50 degrees. There was no understanding it really. The winter would fade easily into spring without much distinction and until you looked at a calendar there was no telling what month you were in at any given moment. Today was one of those chilly days where you wanted to go outside and take the day off, all bundled up.

Sadly, it wasn't meant to be for Amelia. She loved her job that wasn't the issue. What she loved more was her Nana and truth be told she didn't feel like she was doing much good. She loved the freedom her job gave her. She was a guardian and legal consultant for D.S.S. She traveled all of the time. She would often spend her days in Charleston then to Myrtle Beach.

Sometimes she would have a chance to go north for a few days. Wherever her work needed her, she would go. She loved working on each case, and was always thrilled when she felt like she was really helping a family. So many children were always left scared and alone. She could never go back, but she could move forward with change.

Today she was in Myrtle Beach meeting with a family, two children and abusive parents. It never got any easier when she met them for the first time. It just certainly helped when they gave her a smile. She took a deep breath and went through the double doors to the lobby where she would meet the children and the attorneys. He felt like he was somehow responsible for the entire mess. Each board member was currently looking down their respective noses at him across the table.

"Look Jacob, we understand this is a ...um... situation, however we have to follow protocol. I've managed to get with the investigation team and they are looking into the mess. I've heard you have a meeting with the Randolph family and I think you need to reel that in for us."

The comment came from Brandon Workman. He had been there as long as his father had.

"Listen, Workman I get what you're saying, I'm just not sure why I am the only dealing with P.R. Do we not have a team for that? I have my own business issues to work out with the Landowe project." A few of the people at the table glanced at each other and then to the table.

"Well, I'll be honest with you Jake, you're the spokesperson for these types of situations. You're the charmer, the good-looking guy. A situation like this takes finesse and strategy." He had the decency to blush slightly.

"Let me get this straight, I am the CEO and I am also a part-time playboy schmoozes the ladies in my off time?" He sat back in a huff.

Workman looked around the table at the other members before settling on Jacob again. "Well, yes so to speak. Your father was the same way before you. You both have that ability to put people at ease." He smiled slightly, the noisy throat clearing around the room didn't go unnoticed either.

"You mean with the women." He gave Workman a half smile. He was the voice of reason around here after all. "Fine I'll go at it alone, but I need some real results from the testing site before I walk into whatever mess comes with the Randolph lady."

Amelia stared at herself in the mirror in her old room. Today was going to be a long day. She was certain of that, and not much else. She had taken great care to look nice. Her hair was twisted up on the back of her head, her make-up was subtle and effective and she wore a nice suit and skirt. It fit her just right. She wore pumps, something she rarely did and she had a firm set to her jaw. Today she would get some answers. She stood and squared her shoulders and took a few deep breaths.

It was just like going into a new home. She would listen, make her assessment and they would go from there. She made her way down to the car and drove into town. It was a lenghty ride into Charleston, just long enough that she could take in some deep breaths along the way and try to stop her heart from beating out of her chest. It would serve no purpose if she lost her temper, no matter what she had to stay calm.

She climbed the front stairs of the building and looked up at the massive structure. She shook her head. Who needed that much space for anything? It was all too much really. She entered and gave her name to the guard who patted her down with a wink and she was finally in the elevator going up. She heard a shout and she noticed a man running towards her so she thrust her hand out to stop the elevator. He slid into the elevator and took a deep breath.

"Wow, I barely made it that time, thanks." He glanced over at her. She was beautiful, her hair was a jumble of colors wound up tightly with the appearance that it would break free at any moment.

"Sure, no problem." She tried not to stare at him. He was reeking of sexiness. He had dark hair slightly unruly and blue eyes that felt like they could look a hole right through you. He was tall, very tall and impeccably dressed. She self-consciously ran her hands down over her skirt. She could feel him watching her and she finally turned to look at him.

"Is there something on my face or something?" She noticed his surprise and then the grin that slid into its place."No, not at all, you're just beautiful, that's all." It was his turn to get a rise out of her. He saw the blush creep up her neck and into her face."Whatever." She rolled her eyes and stared back at the elevator, watching intently as it made its slow accent to the top floor. "You are, but I have to say it is refreshing."

He failed to elaborate as the doors opened and he stepped out. "I hope to see you again." He whistled as he strode away from the elevator, leaving her wondering what he was talking about.

Men were crazy, that much she was sure of. Finally the elevator climbed the last few floors and she exited it into a massive waiting area. There was a coffee bar on one end of the room which looked like a small café. She couldn't believe the excess that people used. She made her way to the receptionist desk and gave her name.

"Randolph, you said Miss?"

"Yes, that's right." She noticed the receptionist glance around a bit before buzzing back to Mr. Montgomery's office.

"Yes, ok, yes that's fine, I'll let her know." She had glanced up at Amelia a few times before hanging up.

"Mr. Montgomery is on his way here now and as soon as he arrives I'll send you back."

With a huff, Amelia made her way over to an overstuffed chair in the lobby. He wasn't even there yet. The whole thing was ridiculous. He was probably on some yacht somewhere while her grandmother was lying in a hospital sick. She felt the tension rising and she hoped he would get there soon before anything else happened.

Jacob made his way up the stairs to his office. She had been a real beauty that one. She was gorgeous, but in an unrefined way and she was direct, something many people never were in his life, it made him like her even more. He was kicking himself for not getting her name at the very least. For now he would just have to hope he would run into her again soon. She was in his building how hard could it be to find one woman?

He gathered up some paperwork from his desk and made his way over to the conference room. The receptionist had already called him ten minutes ago and told him, Amelia Randolph was there. He knew what kind of morning as ahead of him, but he had exited the elevator a couple of floors down so that he could sneak up the back way.

He didn't need to be attacked in his own lobby. He quickly scanned the paperwork in his hands regarding the water testing site and frowned. This was not going to be a good meeting. At least he had chosen a conference room in the corner of the floor where they wouldn't be bothered, or heard. Reluctantly, he buzzed up front and told the girl to bring her in.

It was ridiculous how long someone had to wait for a meeting. The lack of attendance only solidified her opinion of Jacob Montgomery. If he had been a real gentleman, if he cared, he would have at least been on time. Finally, the blonde called her name and escorted her to a room at the far side of the building. When she entered, she simply stared at the blonde shut the door.

"You! Really? Did you know it was me or do you always say things like that to people in an elevator?" She crossed her arms and stared at him as he stood. Equally stunned, and a little disappointed he thrust his hand out to her. "No, I didn't know it was you Miss Randolph." He gestured for her to take a seat.

She was upset, she'd be lying is she said that the mystery guy from the elevator had made her feel that warm fuzzy feeling you get deep down. To find out he was that ass, Montgomery she had been dreading squashed any thoughts she'd had while waiting in the lobby. To think, she actually hoped to run into him again, so she could apologize for being so gruff and to figure out what he meant by those last words. Now she was sitting face to face with him.

It was difficult to think straight with her sitting there staring at him. She was all fire and ice at the same time and he was intrigued. There was simply no way the squawking shrill voice on the voicemails could belong to this woman. He shook his head and decided to get down to business.

"Miss Randolph, I am glad we were able to get together finally. I understand you have concerns over the new water treatment plant we have put in and I assure you I am working hard to figure out where the problem is." He sat forward looking at her intently.

"Listen, I know you think your gonna just give me some BS about the plant and how great it is. I don't want to hear any of that. The fact of the matter is people are getting sick, or in the hospital. Something is wrong and I am just here to find out what you are going to do about it before I start asking people myself." She leaned up in her chair meeting him eye to eye.

He almost couldn't stand it. She was on fire, and beautiful. He would be amused watching her come to life if it were in any other situation. He was not used to women like this, so full of fire. Typically, a woman would be a hellcat from time to time, but that was in the bedroom. If they started out like this he could only imagine... Damn, he was getting sidetracked.

"I don't think you need to start asking anyone else, Miss Randolph. The fact of the matter is we have men down there working on it now. The most recent tests I have right here." He pushed the papers over to her. "As you can see there is nothing showing that the mineral content is above average. Although the levels are normal at the plant I am still concerned about why this happened to you. I have no intention of letting it go until I am sure we have fixed the problem, if there is one."

"All I know is that my Nana was fine and then the day after the water was running through your plant she started getting sick. She had been in the hospital three times and each time it's after she goes home and starts using your water." She pointed her finger at him for emphasis.

"I understand, Miss Randolph and I assure you there is nothing I won't do to make this right, for you." His eyes glittered at her dangerously as he emphasized the "for you." She felt the heat rush through her as he watched her. She cleared her throat and glanced back down at the paperwork on the able.

"This paperwork can say whatever it wants, the truth of the matter is something is wrong and I intend to find out what it is." She stood now and he rose with her.

"Fine, meet me at the plant tomorrow morning." He wasn't even sure what possessed him to say it. He knew very little about the mechanics of the plant itself, but he did have a full knowledge of the filtration system.

"What." She crossed her arms over her chest as she looked up at him.

"Tomorrow, meet me at the plant. I'll go take a look around myself and if you're there you can see things as they develop." He crossed his arms and the two of them stood facing each other for a long moment.

The whole thing was dangerous. She knew before she agreed that this was going to go badly. Despite the anger she held at the company, she was attracted to him. She hated herself for it. He stood casually waiting for her to give him an answer. He was probably used to women throwing themselves at him all the time and she would be damned if she was one of them. He was off limits and she needed to turn off whatever attraction she had. He was just a stuffy suit running a business that hurt her Nana. With renewed spirit, she looked up at him.

"Fine, I'll meet you there, what time." She said it with a deadly calm. Almost as if she was someone else. He didn't like this side of her, it made him take a step back.

"9 sharp. Does that work for you?" He took a small step towards her and watched the blush start to creep back up again. She felt it too, he was sure of it. "Sure, that's fine." She turned to leave and opened the door to the room and stopped as he called her name. "Yes?"

"Don't be late." He grinned as she shut the door with a bang and made her way out of the office.

Jacob Montgomery was a jerk, a total and unmistakable jerk. Not only that, he was arrogant and self-serving, just thinking about the way he stood there, arms crossed without a care in the world made her want to scream. She rammed the car into gear and pulled out and headed to the hospital. She was still angry when she arrived.

Who did he think he was giving her orders anyway? She was a grown woman, almost as tall as he was and he thought he could just tell her what to do. Her family was the victim here. He was a bully, yes, that was it. He was just like those kids at the children's home who would give her grief the first year especially. They threw their weight around, uncaring about anyone else. Yep! Jacob Montgomery was a no-good bully! She walked into her Nana's room to find her sitting up and chatting happily with the nurse.

"Nana you look great!" Her anger was gone in an instant. The turnaround was almost unbelievable. Yesterday she had looked so sick still and in the two nights she had been here she had done a complete turnaround.

"Amelia sweetheart, come give me a hug." She raised her arms up and Amelia hugged her tightly. She was so scared. Whenever she got better and went home, the next time it would be worse.

"You must feel better Nana, I'm so glad. Every time you go home it makes you sick. It's that damn water system and I am working on getting it taken care of."

"Now, now Amelia we don't know that for sure yet." She patted Amelia's hand lovingly and leaned back into her pillows. "I may look better, but I am terribly weak still. What have you been up to today, dear you are all dressed up?" She snuggled back into her pillow and shut her eyes momentarily.

"I had a meeting that's all. I met with Montgomery, to hash out things about the plant." She whispered it, in hopes Nana wouldn't really hear everything she said.

Her Nana's eye fluttered open. "You what! Oh, Amelia it won't do it you get yourself all worked up. You know as well as I do that if you push too far you're going to get into trouble. Plus, we all know what happens with that temper of yours." She closed her eyes again, but not before giving Amelia a "You know what I mean" look.

"Yes, Nana I know all about my temper. In my defense, though I don't really get too upset unless I have a real reason to." She humbly looked down and started fighting with a string on the comforter covering the bed.

"Amelia, sweetheart, don't misunderstand I love all your fire, but just last week you made the poor paperboy cry." She gave a slight giggle before folding her hands over her lap.

"He was throwing the paper in the rose bushes Nana, how on earth can you climb in there and get it!"

Nana simply opened her eyes and gave Amelia a knowing glance. "I know, dear." She patted her hand one last time and Amelia watched as she was soon fast asleep.

Amelia sighed, it wasn't a lie. Her temper often got in her way. She liked to think that she was just passionate about certain things. Her work, her Nana and what was right. Besides, most of the time she was loud, but not angry. There was such a lack of common sense in some people she simply couldn't help herself. She made her way across the room and opened her tablet to look at her schedule.

She had a new family to work with next week, but the rest of this week she was free. She hadn't broached the subject of Nana coming to stay with her in her apartment yet. She knew it would be a fight.

Nana loved her house. It was where she and Harold had lived right after they got married and she had never stayed away from there unless she was in the hospital or when she had come to see Amelia graduate college in Maryland. It wasn't that she didn't understand.

The house had been here over half of her life. It was where she had learned to love, learned to trust again. It would always be a part of her life. She had to have Nana closer so that she could watch her more, be there if she needed anything.

Besides, her apartment was on the city water system in Ridgeville, not on the new "system" purchased from Montgomery Enterprises in Daniel Island. She could keep her safe if she would move in. She folded up her table and rested her head against the chair. She let her mind unravel the day's events and found herself fuming once more over the words of Jacob Montgomery.

She decided to get a room in town for the next few nights. It might be a huge expense, but she needed to be there early tomorrow, and the water was still in question at her Nana's, where she had been staying. She said her goodnights to Nana and made her way to a small and efficient hotel along the water. She had always enjoyed Charleston.

Even as a child she had loved the water, even when there was such a chill in the air like tonight. It was only mid-November and yet with temperatures like this maybe they would get some snow this year. The thought made her smile and think back about the snow when she had moved into Nana's house so long ago.

It was a long ride. It must have taken hours to get to the little white house, she was standing in front of. She looked up at the nice lady beside her who had decided to take her home. She took her hand. She was scared, but she didn't want her to know. She had left the girls home and she hoped this was going to be ok.

The nice lady patted the hand in hers and they made their way up the steps. When the door opened, she took a deep breath in of cookies and warm air. She loved being warm and full, both things she knew the nice lady said she never had to worry about again. She watched and waited as the lady locked the door behind her. It was only then that she relaxed.

"I've decided that maybe you should call me Nana. I'm not your mother, but I hope to be there to help you grow up. How does that sound?"

"Nana... I like it." She gave her a toothy smile and walked over towards a big picture on the wall of a man. "Who is he?" She hooked a thumb in the direction of the picture. Nana made her way over to her.

"That was my dear Harold. He went to Heaven a few months ago." She gently touched the picture and then turned to Amelia. "Well, dear are you ready to see your room?"

"I get my own room?" Amelia had gaped at her and followed along behind Nana. When she opened the door, she could just stand there. The entire room was draped in pink and green. There were flowers on the large seat window and she had the softest pink blanket on her bed. There were pillows everywhere and Amelia rushed forward and immediately began to roll around the bed with them, giggling as she did. Nana laughed, pink may have been a bad choice this girl was not about to paint her nails all day she wanted to make a mess.

"The only thing left is to go buy you some clothes, we can do that tomorrow." Amelia ran to hug her close, happy for the first real time in her life. At some point that first night she had been overwhelmed by it all and snuck into Nana's room. She waited but a second before Nana pulled the blankets back. Without a word, she had climbed in and snuggled down in the warmth of the blankets.

The snow came that weekend and the two of them played in the yard and built half of a snowman. She had laughed more in those two days than I her entire life combined. It's how her new life started and now that same chill was in the air tonight. She was still smiling when she put her bags on the floor of her room. She had a nice view and this would be a good way to make efficient use of the time she had. She locked and relocked the door.

A habit of sorts since she was a child. She let her thoughts stray to Evan. She had spent the better part of her career looking for him, some sign of him. She always came up empty. Every lead would bring some closure to another family, but never hers. She decided to take a shower and start prepping for her day tomorrow. There was no telling what Montgomery had up his sleeve.

So far, all Jacob knew was that she wasn't married, and was adopted. He was scanning every piece of information about Amelia Randolph that he could. He needed to find something to connect them. To get her to relax some when he was around. She was 26, graduated from Maryland University. Worked at DSS on a flexible schedule.

She was practically broke, and had fairly good credit. He scanned her finances and noticed she spent a great deal of money looking for someone named Evan Hollinger. Whoever he was, she really wanted him found. Prior to age 12 there were no records for her. He sat back in his chair and spun to look out the window. Something about her fascinated him. Sure, she was beautiful, but that wasn't it.

He had been around beautiful women most of his life. Something wholesome about her made him want to know more. Whatever it was he was not giving up. He was used to getting and doing what he wanted and he wasn't going to start losing at the game now. She was all fire, and all talk. He would find a way to reach her and when he did, he would enjoy their time together. He smiled to himself before heading to take a shower.

The next morning was cold and gray. There was a bitter chill in the air that was hard to shake off. Amelia knew she needed to bundle up and she chose some casual clothes for the day. Denim and an oversized white sweater as well as her knee-high leather boots. She put on her coat and hat, leaving her hair down for the extra layer of warmth. She glanced at the clock and swore. She was never late, ever. Why today of all days did she have to rush? She hastily grabbed her purse and made her way to her car. She didn't even have time for coffee that certainly added to her mood. She climbed in and turned the car over and nothing happened. She tried again.

"Really?" She said it out loud. The car had been giving her issues for a while now, but it was not the day. Of all days, not the day.

She jumped out of the car and shut her door with a bang. Now she would have to call someone and try and get the thing towed over to a garage. She hastily called Montgomery Enterprises.

After ten minutes of dealing with some snotty girl she passed on her message. He was probably laughing at her misfortune and happy she wouldn't be there to get in the way. She kicked the curb on her way back into her room and waited to hear from him.

Oh man, she was going to be angry, he smiled slightly thinking about her reaction. He wouldn't doubt it if she was kicking in the side of her car right now. He hung up his phone and looked around the penthouse for his coat. He decided to try and get on her good side and so he sent her a text asking where she was staying.

Perhaps there was some way he could put her back in a good mood before he arrived. He made his way downstairs and to his personal car. He liked to venture out on his own sometimes and today was the perfect day for it. He glanced up at the sky and frowned. It was probably going to snow later today. They weren't going to have much time if he didn't hurry. He pulled out onto the highway and made his way into town.

She was puzzled by his message, at least she assumed it was him. It wasn't like he had said "hey, it's Montgomery." She was frustrated by the whole situation and her lack of expertise when it came to cars. She needed to take a class or something. This was an awful situation to be in.

She saw him pull up before she even looked at who was driving. The red sports car was sleek and shiny and she knew it could only belong to Montgomery. She walked towards him from the lobby as he got out. He was handsome in black denim and a polo shirt. He had on a black coat and gloves, which he took off as he made his way over to her. He even had a sexy sway to his walk. She rolled her eyes, disgusted with herself.

He tried to gauge her mood as he made his way over to her. She had her arms crossed again, a sure sign she wasn't happy. Her jeans were tight, perfectly tight. She had rounded hips, he wanted to touch and her mane of hair flowed down past her shoulders. He wondered what it would feel like if he put his hands in it. Instead, he gave her a smile.

"I figured I could just pick you up and we go together. Saves time and gas."

"You could have told me you were coming. Or said who you were when you text me, you know?"

"Sorry, I was in a hurry." He frowned at her slightly. She really was always in a foul mood. "If you're coming I suggest we get going." He turned and headed towards his car.

She felt bad immediately. What was wrong with her, she was never this short tempered. She followed him to the car and slid into the seat, buckling up as he shut her door for her. She waited until she was inside before addressing the topic at hand.

"Listen Montgomery, I'm sorry. I don't know what's wrong with me. I'm just so concerned about Nana. This car situation just pushed me over. I appreciate the ride, really." She gave him a quick glance as he buckled up.

"My pleasure, and please call me Jacob. Using my last name reminds me of high school football. I don't want to revisit that." He grimaced slightly and she smiled.

They made their way to the water treatment plant near Daniel Island. It had been a huge undertaking for the company and he had overseen every aspect of the project. He had educated himself about the filtration process, but he wished now that he had learned more about the engineering of it. It was a gleaming metal unit attached on one side to the building that held the support offices and the staff who maintained it.

They made their way down and into the building. She had never been this close to it before and was in awe at the mechanics that went into running something of this magnitude. He asked for Benjamin Astre, the manager of the plant and they were quickly greeted by a round man with a face as red as an apple. His happiness was almost infectious as he pumped both of their hands and led them into a control room. Most of what he said made no sense to her, but she took in every aspect of the system and how it worked.

"This channel here, do they lead strictly to Daniels Island or does it cover something else as well?" Both men turned her way and Benjamin answered.

"This filtration channel strictly runs to Daniels, more specifically the smaller end of Beresfor Creek. You can see the larger system pumps into the larger area of Beresford and then branches to Nowell Creek."

She looked over the system more before following them down towards the actual filtering controls. If the filtering channel ran strictly to Daniels Island than the issue would have to be central to that one run. She moved towards the huge pumping filters. They were massive and connected the water in the creeks into the system and then back into the holding tanks that would then pump water to the homes where they were directed. The whole set up was beautiful, even if it was making people sick.

"I have set up something for you both. I understand that there has been some concern on your part Miss Randolph about the water content. I have some instruments here, and if you would like to I'd be happy to allow you both to take your own samples and run them through the testing equipment. I think this could help with what you're looking for."

She smiled at him and readily agreed. They spent the next two hours moving and testing water both filtered and unfiltered. They talked about life in general, her work and his and she found that he really wasn't too bad to spend time around after all. He was still a rich snob, and a bully, but he wasn't as bad as she originally thought.

He was feeling the same way. She was a strong and smart woman and, unlike most women he knew, she didn't care that her clothes were wet and messy. She was on a mission and was all businesslike about it. She needed to know the truth. He loved the tinkling sound her laugh made when she wasn't trying so hard to be stern. He wanted to kiss her, right there with water spraying on them in the frigid air.

Even in these temperatures he was on fire thinking about it, about her. Eventually they were done and what they found left them both puzzled. There was no indication of any levels of negative or harmful properties in the water. What was being sent into Daniels Island was as pure as it could come.

What bothered him was the lack of an Hd5 filter he had specifically asked for on the system. It hadn't been put on the system and he had a pretty good idea why. The bored had fought him on the cost. They both left the plant lost in thought. After an audible sigh coming from her he glanced her way. She was upset and visibly so.

"I know you wanted, needed even, something to be there in that water. I had it tested over and over again. I also know, given your personality you wouldn't believe me unless you did the testing yourself."

"What do you mean my personality? Contrary to what you may think I am a very pleasant person to be around." He gave her a look with a half grin and she knew she was delivering him exactly what he had been referring to.

"Yeah, okay, I get it, I can be... difficult. It's just Nana, it doesn't make any sense at all Jacob. She is fine then goes home and then is sick again and everything they test at the hospital says it's in something she drinks. She only drinks water, I know that for a fact. That's all she has ever drank." She tapped her fingers on her lips in thought.

"I'm not sure what it is, but I'll continue to keep digging. I like it when you're not angry at me." He smiled at her again.

She felt the heat rising in her face. He had the most unusual ability to make her blush. She usually had a firm control on it. He turned left as they entered town and she frowned. This was not the way to the hotel. She felt the panic start building and she gripped the handle of the car door.

"Where are we going?" She gritted out the words. He turned to see her white faced and gripping the door. What was wrong?

"Hey, you ok? I was going to stop off for lunch, that's all. There is a diner right there see?" He pointed ahead and she could see the building. She relaxed and pulled her hand off the door handle.

"That's great, I'm starving." She gave him a weak smile and he frowned. Something was not right and he intended to find out what it was.

She excused herself to go to the bathroom once they were inside. She splashed some water on her face fighting the tears she didn't want to come. When would she ever stop being afraid? It wasn't often, but when the panic would set in, it was hard to shake off. Jacob wasn't going to hurt her, she knew that.

There was something about the day Evan had disappeared and the way the man had grabbed her. If he hadn't come along she might have made it home. She stood and used a paper towel to blot dry her face. She pushed her mass of hair back and pinched her cheeks for color.

She frowned slightly. Was she really in here primping for Jacob Montgomery? She turned and made her way into the restaurant.

He noticed the color had returned to her face as she sat down. He continued to watch her as she ordered food and he gave her a smile once he had done the same. They made random small talk and he smiled again.

"What are you smiling at Jacob?" she leaned forward in the booth slightly.

"Nothing at all Amelia, I am appreciative of how you do things that's all."

She frowned again, that didn't sound very promising. "What do you mean how I do things?"

"I'm just used to women being a certain way that's all. I like you better." He flashed a smile at her again and she blushed.

"What's wrong with me that I'm not like other women?" The words were no sooner out of her mouth and the waitress delivered the food. She looked down at the massive meal before her. Chiliburger, fries, milkshake and cherry pie. She took a gulp and blushed as she looked up at him, "Point taken." His laughter was loud and she joined in with him.

"You are too much Amelia." He wiped at his eyes and started to attack the food on his side.

They hadn't been eating long when a leggy blond came into the diner. She gave a once over around the room until she found who she was looking for. Amelia knew trouble when she spotted it and this was definitely going to go badly.

The blond stopped at the table and made eye contact with Amelia. The two instantly disliked each other. The air surrounding the blond was enough to make you choke. She held her head up high and had a disgusted look on her face as she glanced around at the other patrons in the room.

"Jacob, darling." She said it sweetly and he gave a start as he glanced up at her.

"Jessalyn, wow, what are you doing here?" He stood up quickly and glanced over at Amelia.

"I called the office and they said you were stopping here on your way back, I had to see you darling, and something important has come up." She looked down her nose at Amelia before adding. "Darling, what are you doing in a place like this?"

He gritted his teeth and introduced the two. "Jessalyn this is Amelia, Amelia, Jessalyn."

"Nice to meet you." Amelia managed to get out. She received a half smile from her counterpart.

"Jessalyn, now is not a good time we are working on some business together and I'm driving."

"Really Jacob we need to talk, it looks like there is another person here with you," she gestured at all the food on the table, "Can they not take her home, I really need to chat with you." She felt the sting of the words and noticed he had the decency to look angry.

Before he had a chance to make it worse, she decided to chime in. "Jacob its fine, I can find my way to the hotel, it's just around the corner. Go its fine." She leaned back in the chair, noticing the pained look on his face.

"No, it's not right here." He threw her his keys. "Drive it to your hotel and I'll come get it later. I'll just ride with her." Before she could turn him down he left and escorted blondie with him.

It wasn't really about what she said. It was really about how this woman was the type Jacob was obviously interested in. She never wanted to be like that. She would take her jeans and a chili burger every day of the week before she would show up and look down her nose at the world. She finished her lunch and decided to take the sports car for a ride to the hospital. The rest of the evening flew by for them both.

Jacob's head was reeling and he wasn't sure what he was going to do. Jessalyn had come back here just to tell him she may be pregnant. The last thing he needed was a baby with a woman he didn't love. It changed his entire thought process. If it was his of course he would be a good father. There was nothing more important than that. She was going to the doctor tomorrow and then he would know what was going on.

He looked over at his clock. 8 pm. Amelia was probably wondering when he was coming to get his car. He loved that car, he was still surprised he had given her the keys. He tried to call her but no answer. He smiled. She had been carefree and relaxed. He liked her that way. Whatever had caused her to panic in the car is what concerned him. Something wasn't right there and he decided to look into it. He sat forward and opened his computer.

Her back was killing her. All she could think of was the pain she was feeling and her eyes flew open to investigate the culprit. She was draped across the chair in Nans room and the blanket someone had draped over her had twisted itself into the nuisance currently digging into her back. She glanced at the clock and yawned. It was 10 o'clock. She needed to get back to the hotel.

She felt around the table for her keys and frowned at the weight of them. Suddenly her eyes opened wide. She still had his car. Damn. She jumped up carefully tiptoeing out of the room and rushed out to the car. She slipped into his cool leather seats. It was only then that she noticed the snow was falling. She grabbed around for her phone and noticed he had called. She decided to text him in case he was asleep.

"Fell asleep, sorry. Your car is at my hotel whenever you want it."

She carefully made her way through town with a smile on her face as the snow fell gently in waves. She had just pulled into a spot and jumped out when she heard something behind her. She stopped.

"Hey beautiful come hang out with me." He was drunk and walking towards her car. He was halfway between her and the hotel. She grabbed her purse and started to run past him. He reached out and grazed her arm and she went into a full panic. She sprinted past him and ran into something hard and warm. She looked up and Jacob was the last thing she saw before she fainted.

Warmth. She always loved it. She snuggled down into the blankets and sighed. She had been having the most wonderful dream about Jacob kissing her. Jacob! She sat up with a start. The last thing she remembered was looking up at him.

"Hey there sleepyhead." He was comfortably draped out in a chair beside her bed and reading through some paperwork. She looked over at the clock. It had only been an hour since she left the hospital.

"What happened? What happened to that man did he leave?" She was frantic now and shaking like a leaf. He walked towards her and wrapped her in a hug.

"He is gone, Amelia, I called the police and he is gone." He felt her relax in his arms. She smelled like lavender.

He wanted nothing more than to stay just like this. She raised her head to look at him and it was more than he could take. He crushed his mouth to hers. Tasting and exploring. He had wanted to kiss her since the elevator and it was better than he had expected. He felt her let go and he deepened the kiss. He slid both hands into her hair and pulled her head closer still. They fed on each other's lips until finally the kiss broke.

He stared at her, wanting her. He couldn't remember a time in his life where he wanted someone more. She was panting, having been as rocked by the kiss as he was. Not like this, he wanted her but not because she was vulnerable. He stood and walked over to the window. The snow was falling and it was getting deeper by the moment. If he didn't leave now he would be stuck here.

"Jacob, are you going to leave? You don't have too, if you don't want to." She wasn't sure if she was motivated by fear or desire. She just didn't want him to leave.

"I don't want to leave, Amelia. I'm rarely one for doing the right thing, trust me." He glanced over at her. "You've had a rough night, I don't want to take advantage of you. When we make love, I want it to be because you want to." The last words he spoke as he looked at her.

She needed no other convincing. She wanted him. He had been there for her, and stayed to make sure she was ok. He had helped her try to find out the problem with the water. He had been there. She stood beside the bed and took off her pants as he watched her.

She climbed back onto the bed on her knees and pulled her shirt over the top of her head. She rid herself of the rest of her clothing quickly and he was afraid to move. She was perfect, if he moved he was afraid he would ruin it somehow. He managed to say her name through gritted teeth.

"Amelia, are you sure?" At her nod, he quickly made his way over to her. He covered her in kisses and so started a night they would never forget.

The sun was almost angry. That was the only thing she could think of at the intrusive way it beamed in on her. She glanced at the clock and was shocked it was 9 am. She never slept this late. She tried to sit up and felt the chill in the air. Suddenly the previous night flooded her memory. She looked around her. She was in a tangled mess of sheets, and she was alone. She wrapped one around her and made her way over to a note on the table.

"Be back soon, getting breakfast. Shower. We need to talk." J

She smiled as she made her way to the shower. Gone were the fears of the night before. She knew she would have to explain it all to him in time. She frowned, in time? She would be a fool to think this was anything more than a one-time thing. Especially after meeting "blonde and leggy" yesterday.

This was just one of those things that happened. He probably thought she was some slut anyway since they had only met this week. She shrugged, she owned everything she did, good or bad. She showered and dressed quickly waiting for him to return.

A mile away Jacob was all smiles. Jessalyn was not pregnant, and he was falling for a red-haired siren. He had gotten the call while waiting for the food to take back to the hotel and he was relieved. He really wanted to focus on where this was going with Amelia.

He had never felt so alive, so free. He made his way back to the hotel carrying the food when he noticed the men working on the pipes beside the diner they had visited just the day before. He stopped the car and a thought occurred to him. With a huge smile, he made his way up to her room.

"Amelia... you in there?" He knocked on the door and pulled her into his arms as she opened it. He put the food on the table and grabbed her hand. "We have to go, come on." She was confused. What was he running all crazy about? He was on his way back out and noticed she was only half dressed and had a head full of wet hair. She noticed him taking in her appearance.

"Yeah, so I was thinking I could finish getting dressed first and then you can tell me what's got you so worked up." She moved to slide on her jeans and he watched her every move. He was fascinated by her.

"Sorry, I get excited sometimes. I think I have an answer for you, first let's eat. There is snow everywhere and you need to eat."

"Yeah, because I'm so skinny I may just float away." She said it with sarcasm and a smile.

"I don't like skinny, I like curves." He glanced at her and crossed his arms, "You'll do." She threw a pillow at him as she wound her hair up in a ponytail and sat down to eat a quick breakfast.

"So, you have an answer about what?" She sipped her coffee and ate her food.

"Oh no, it's a surprise, just eat and we will go." He gave her a huge smile as she licked her fingers clean. She was adorable.

"What?" She shrugged. He handed her a coat and they made their way to the car.

As they rode along, she thought it was a good time to bring up last night." Jacob listen. Last night was great. I don't want you to worry I will be expecting anything. I hope we can be friends and everything." She watched the trees fly by as she said it.

"What are you talking about? Expect anything? This isn't high school, Amelia.

"I'm just saying..."

"I know exactly what you're saying." He cut her off and she frowned. She had given him an out, and he was pissed. She glanced back out the window and frowned, they were headed to her Nana's house, she was sure of it. He made the final turn and pulled into the driveway of her childhood home." Jacob, what are we doing here?" She got out and waited as he pulled a large bag out of the trunk.

"I was thinking, your Nana was getting sick when she was at home drinking, but the water tested fine at the plant. The only solution is the pumping system here at the house."

They made their way around the house to the old water cover and pump. She knew factually it hadn't been changed or looked at in at least 12 years. He pulled the cover off the system and turned on the water directly coming out of the pipe. He put some in a vial and put two drops of something in it and shook. It took less than a minute before theater turned a dark blue color.

"I knew it, the lead levels are through the roof. The problem is the system outside the house Amelia."

She took the vial from him in awe. All this time she had been coming after him and the problem was, literally, in the backyard. She made her way inside and he followed. She sat at the kitchen table and rested her head in her hands. Now she would get it fixed, and everything would go back to normal.

"How much does one of those things cost?" She glanced over at him as he looked around her old room. "It varies really, not too much." He smiled at her.

"Listen, I don't know what I said earlier, but I was trying to make it easy for you to walk away, you get that right?" She crossed her arms over her chest. Something she had done many times before.

"Amelia, I don't want to be let off the hook, I want you, I want to be there for you when it gets hard, I want to eat chili burgers together and be close if you panic again, and you don't have to be scared of anything ever again." He took a step towards her and she frowned.

"What are you talking about? Panic again or scared anymore?" She looked up at him and her face fell. "Did you look up information about me, Jacob?"

He looked scared before he answered. "Yes, but I wanted to get to know you that's all I didn't know about, everything you had been through."

"So you found out all about me and then slept with me? What was the reason, pity?" She was loud now, angry and crying.

"Amelia, no, it's not like that. He took a step towards her."

She stopped him, "Go Jacob, just go. NOW!"

Nothing left to say he made his way outside and spun his tires as he headed back to Charleston.

She had been back to work two weeks now. She tried to take on every case she could, to help take her mind off of things. Two weeks since she had seen him. He was still texting and calling and she refused to acknowledge any of it. He had betrayed her. She looked up from her desk.

Tonight she would go see her Nana and check on the new system she had purchased with a new credit card. It would take at least a year to pay it off, but it was worth it. She made her way to her car and set off for Daniel Island.

This had to work, he had tried everything else and yes, it was sneaky getting Nana in on it but she wouldn't respond to him. He was in love with her and she loved him too, if she would stop being so stubborn.

He had hurt her, he knew that now, but he couldn't make it right if she avoided him.

He glanced over at Nana who was rocking happily in her chair. They had talked for hours about Amelia and she knew he loved Amelia very much. She had shared so much about Amelia he loved her even more than he had before. He stood when he heard the car pull up. She was going to be furious, and he knew it.

"She will only be mad for a moment son, she is always more bark than bite." Nana chuckled to herself.

The door opened and she came in with an armful of bags. "Nana what in the hell is that monstrosity out back? I didn't pay for that and I hope they don't think I'm going to. That model was $5,000 more dollars than the one I got you. Not that I don't want you to have the best but ..." She trailed off as she turned and saw him there.

"Don't get mad, don't say anything until I'm done Amelia." He glanced at Nana who gave him an encouraging nod. Amelia stood frozen to the spot. "I am in love with you Amelia Randolph and I probably was from the first day we met. I know what I did was wrong, I'm sorry if I hurt you. The truth is we belong together.

You help me be a better man and I'll force you to go to society balls and spend a lot of money on charities and things you will hate doing, but you will do it because you love me. I want to spend my life with you Amelia, and I want to face challenges together. I want to help you find Evan."

He looked over at her and the tears streaming down her face. Good or bad he wasn't sure yet. Nana, who always loved a good love story sat up on the edge of her seat and waited. With a sob Amelia threw herself into his arms and relished in the feel of him holding her. This was where she belonged. She looked up at him.

"That monstrosity out there I bought for Nana. She deserved the best. She brought us together, it was the least I could do." He gave Nana a grin and she just shooed him away. He hugged her close.

"Do you remember in the elevator that day, I said it was refreshing?" He smiled.

"Yes, what did you mean exactly?" She pulled away slightly.

"I meant it was refreshing to meet a woman who was beautiful and didn't even know it." He leaned in for a kiss.

****

The Bad Boy's Wish

Braden Davenport was on cloud nine. Even now, as he pulled off his helmet, he felt great. He was on a streak and this was going to be his best season yet. He brushed his hand through his jet-black hair and smiled at the people around him. It was nice having fans. They were the only constant in his life, always there to cheer him on. The problem was, they didn't really know him.

That's not to say that it isn't great doing what you love for a living. He was able to buy his first house at the age of 23, and at 29, he owned three. He liked to have a nice place to stay whenever he was in his favorite places. Racing was a dangerous sport, but it was in his blood, a part of him. Being here in Austin for the MotoGP race had been a fluke, but a happy one. He was a last minute add in and he was happy he said yes.

He would always rather be racing than home alone or out with some nameless girl that didn't know him very well. For now, he was home in Texas, at least for the next two months. It was the place where this all began and he was happy to be there. He loved the dry air and the open grounds in the hill country, and the city life in Austin. His next race was in Vegas and he was happy for the break. The win today would put enough money in the bank that he could live off forever, but it was never enough. Having lived such a hard life growing up, he liked the better, secure, lifestyle he had now.

He basically lived his life in an orphanage. He never knew his father, who left his mother soon after he was born. His mother was heartbroken and soon became an addict. He still remembered what it was like finding her there when he was 7. She made the wrong person mad, and they gave her some bad stuff. He found her unresponsive, lying on the living room floor. They didn't have a phone, but fortunately he was able to run to a neighbor and they called the police for him. He still carried around the guilt because he couldn't save her. He eventually left the orphanage and made a few friends. He had a difficult time trusting people, getting close to anyone.

He got his first job at the thrift store in town. He learned the hard way that life was about making the right choices or you end up with nothing. Over time, he managed to secure a room, and that's when he met Gerald and Abbie Smith. Older, they were frequent shoppers where he worked, and they always amused him. At 80, Gerald was a big bear of a man. Abbie was a tiny little thing at 77. Abbie would tell Braden he looked too thin, and Gerald would pull him aside and talk cars with him, something he always loved. After a year or so, they invited him to dinner. At 19, he still seemed like a kid to Abbie. She was always fussing over him and making sure he actually ate when he came over.

Gerald was the person who taught Braden to race. He owned many bikes, he was a collector of sorts, and the moment Braden rode one, his life changed. He maneuvered them like a pro. After some help from Gerald's contacts, he quickly became successful and was able to secure himself a lucrative future in racing. When Braden was 21, Gerald passed away, and Abbie followed a year later. He moved in to help her after Gerald's passing, and held her hand when she died.

That was seven years ago now, and he could still remember it like it was yesterday. He shook his head, remembering, and smiled. He made sure his bike was always in tip top shape, and made frequent visits to his trusted mechanic and best friend, Mike's house. They met in his early years of racing, and had been friends ever since.

The most important thing that Gerald taught Braden was that the bike is your money and the only way you can ride it safely is if you have a hand in what goes on with it. The bike was his family, and he protected it as such. He finally set off for the hour drive to Marble Falls, where Mike lived.

Mike was always a party guy. One girl to the next and one disaster away from an addiction. What he did have was a nice house, and a serious garage behind it. It was the one thing he always took care of. His mother would come over once a month and clean up for him. As he pulled into the parking lot of the townhouses, Braden noticed the changes. The place next door was vacant the last time he was there, and he wondered if Mike even knew that someone had moved in.

He was taking the next few weeks to run off with his newest girlfriend and had given Braden the key so that he could drop some things off, and pick up some things for the bike. He noticed her the moment he pulled up. He watched amused as a plus size woman was desperately trying to get her key to work in her door knob.

"Damn it."

She was angry and she was beautiful. She finally kicked the door and turned to go to her car. She stopped when she saw him watching her. She gave him a half smile before pushing her hair back and squaring her shoulder.

"I'm not usually so easily flustered. My key broke off in the door... now I am rambling sorry... so yeah, I should go." She turned to go again and he finally said something.

"I can probably get that out of there if you want me to try." He crossed his arms as she gave him a half smile.

"That would be... well... yes, please." She smiled at him again and he went to the truck.

BBW Chloe closed her eyes and took a deep breath. She was standing here rambling like an idiot. It always happened when she met a guy, especially an attractive one. Attractive didn't even begin to describe this one. He was, by far, the most attractive guy she had seen in a long time. He had black hair and dark eyes and just enough stubble on his face to give him that mysterious look. She never even kissed a guy like that and she never would. It certainly didn't hurt to watch him though. He was all muscle, and it was obvious he worked out. She blushed as he came back towards her, hopefully he hadn't seen her looking him over like that.

He smiled as he worked on the door. She was looking him over and it made him smile. The fact that she blushed when he looked at her made him like her even more. He finally broke the broken key out and he turned to look at her again. It was her amazing curves and beautiful eyes that struck him first. Her eyes were deep blue and full of life, and they contrasted the abundance of red flowing hair. She was a big girl, and he liked that about her. She had curves in all of the right placed and he wanted to touch every single one of them. He glanced at her hand and didn't see a ring, which was a good first step. He handed her the broken pieces of the key, and when his eyes met hers, he saw her blush again.

"It should be fine now, I had to put some lube in it." He gave her a half smile.

"What... oh thanks." She gathered the pieces up and headed towards the door. "Thanks again..."

"Braden... my name is Braden." He held his hand out to her and she shook it.

"I'm Chloe, nice to meet you."

"Perhaps I can get you to have dinner with me sometime, Chloe?" He watched the myriad of emotions cross her face.

"Sure, that sounds like fun." She turned to head back in again and he smiled.

"Chloe, can I get your number?"

"Oh, sorry." She wrote it down and turned to go again.

She was a flighty one, but that was part of the excitement for him. He watched her go inside and he left, heading for his place in the hills. She was timid, something he would remedy. Even now he thought about her curves and how they would feel under his fingers. He rarely ever lost at this and he didn't intend to start now.

Chloe shut the door with a thud. That was very sweet of him, offering to have dinner with him. It was typical of some guys, nicer ones anyway, to offer to take the big girl out. She didn't need to get paraded around and everyone's opinion of him go up because he did her a favor. Still, he seemed genuine. She made her way into the house and took a good long look at herself in the mirror. She had been working hard to lose weight, to be in better shape. She was down 20 pounds but she still hated the way she looked. Aside from her friends and her little brother, she was alone. In some ways it suited her. She'd had one serious relationship and that left her ready to just put the idea of love and romance behind her for good.

After, she made her way into her room to throw on pajamas and spent the rest of the afternoon cleaning until Charlie got out of school. At 12, he was more than a handful of energy. In a week, he would be gone with friends on vacation, and she would really be alone all summer. He had been living with her a year and a half now, but some days it seemed like only yesterday that he had moved in. She was 22 and ready to tackle the world when she got the call. Her parents and her little brother were in an accident.

Like most people, she didn't think anything could happen to her. She rushed to the hospital, but her parents were both gone, leaving Charlie, with her. It was a rough start, but they were good now. She'd be lying if she said she didn't get lonely sometimes though. He kept her busy, one activity to another. Motherhood at her age was not part of her plan, but she was lucky they had each other. That thought brought her back to Braden. She wondered if he had a family. He seemed like a nice guy.

She never had an opportunity to meet her neighbor. As far as she knew the little lady that came in and out on occasion was the only one who visited that house at all. She sighed, she had rambled on and on about nothing, he must have thought her a complete idiot. Finally, she sat down to calculate how to pull off everything this month.

She was a local teacher, well she was a substitute. She was still in school part-time but she was determined to finish. Most of the time she worked enough days to just barely pay the bills, but having a 12-year-old with numerous after school activities put a dent in things. Not to mention the rent on this place was out outrageous. Since her parents were renting as well, their place was too much for her to take on.

They were always like the traveling circus, always moving and changing. Chloe didn't want that for her little brother. She lived that life and he needed stability. She would simply have to cut out some things, but first she would have to find what those things were.

Braden walked into his house, well Gerald's and Abbie's house. They left it for him in the will. No children of their own, they took him in and loved him as if he were theirs. He didn't live here, it didn't feel like he should, and to be honest, he didn't want to take over. He liked being able to walk in and see their things as they left it. It gave him a sense of peace. Deep down, he knew it wasn't healthy, he should sell it, but for now he couldn't let go.

He checked on things here and then headed to the place he lived in the hills. He called ahead the week before so that it could be opened up and aired out. He hadn't been here in months and knowing it would be ready was one of the many luxuries he enjoyed. He had a house manager and a housekeeper, both trustworthy friends, and he compensated them well for the work they did for him.

Once he was there, he made his way inside and he poured himself a drink, leisurely making his way to the large windows overlooking the city. He wanted her. The thought crossed his mind and he smiled. Chloe, there was something about her that struck a nerve, and he wanted to figure it out. He thought at first it had been her coy and shy personality, but he had played that game before and knew that wasn't it.

There was a depth to her, and he wanted to know more. Women were always around, throwing themselves at him and offering him their charms. It came with the business... and the money. It was rare he felt connected to someone who didn't know about either of those things. She felt the connection too, but she simply dismissed it, and he wanted to know why. He suddenly smiled as an idea came to mind. She had no clue who he was or the money he made. Even in her wildest dream, would she ever guess that he was a billionaire. He pulled out his phone and called Mike.

Braden pulled up to Mike's townhouse once more with a renewed spirit. Mike had given him the green light at least for the next few weeks. That would be plenty of time to figure Chloe out. He glanced over at her place before heading inside. Much like his penthouse, the place hadn't been lived in in months. Everything shined and gleamed. "Thank you, Mrs. Anderson." He said under his breath.

She was a sweet woman, often quiet and reserved, but she could clean the hell out of this bachelor pad. He decided there was no time like the present to start pursuing his curvy neighbor. He made his way over to her door. It wasn't late, so he gave it a knock. She opened the door in a flurry, and as soon as she saw him, she looked shocked.

> "Braden hello." She smiled at him and he felt the heat rising in him. Her hair was pulled up on top of her head and she was wearing a t-shirt and sweats. Casual and damn near the sexiest thing he had ever seen.

> "Hello Chloe, thought I'd see if you were up for a chat? It's just that I've been out of town and it's hard to get resettled." He gave her a smile and gauged her reaction.

She was just a little intimidated. She assumed he would move on and let her be, but here he was, in his tight jeans and arms that looked ready to rip out of his shirt. She gulped slightly, what was wrong with her? She usually had more control over herself than this. She gave him a half smile.

"I wish I could. It's just that my little brother is here and is sleeping." There, that should put him off.

"Oh, I see. Maybe we could sit on the deck?" He shoved his hands in his pockets and she mechanically nodded a yes. He smiled at her again and she moved to let him in.

She must be completely out of her mind. What was she doing? She didn't even know him that well and she just let him walk right into her house. He could be a crazy person or something. She sighed.

"I'm not a killer or anything, if that's what you're worried about." They had made it to the sliding door and he leaned in behind her, whispering it in her ear.

She felt the heat of his breath on her ear and shivered. It had been a long time, very long, and she was just sensitive that's all. They moved out to the deck, and as she shut the door and turned towards him, he was directly in front of her.

"Are you married Chloe?" He leaned towards her as he said it, propping his arm against the sliding door beside her head.

"You're very forward aren't you?" "No, I'm not, said Braden, are you?" She ducked through his arm and made her way over to the wrought iron chairs on the deck. It was dark out there. Having forgotten the deck lights were blown, she silently cursed. She turned around again, and this time he walked over to the rail. She joined him there, waiting and suddenly he turned towards her.

"No, I'm not." He put an arm on either side of her and rested against the railing. As he did so he leaned into her breathing in the scent of jasmine.

She was lost in that moment, He was inches away from her and her only thought was that he must be really desperate to be here with her. More than anything else, she didn't want to look like a fool, it's happened before and she didn't want to go through that again. She dipped below his arm and faced the trees again. She could hear his chuckle, and she frowned.

"You are something else Chloe, you know I want to kiss you, but you keep running, why?"

She looked at him, surprised by his admission. "Why do you want to kiss me? I'm sure you have plenty of other women to kiss, besides, I don't even know you, Braden."

"What better way to get to know me, Chloe." He stood and gave her a smile.

There was something about the way he said it that left her wondering if he was serious or simply out of his mind. She shook her head and turned back around.

"Don't be ridiculous Braden."

She said it simply and he realized she meant it. He frowned as he thought about it. Maybe she wasn't attracted to him. There was only one way to find out. He slid over to the right and grasped her hand in his and pulled her towards him. He saw the look of surprise on her face as he put his hand against the back of her head, pulling her into his arms as his mouth crushed hers.

She was on fire and he did nothing but add fuel to it. She felt his mouth nip at her lips and then dive deeper. She opened her mouth to him, unconsciously meeting his kiss eagerly. As their tongues danced, she felt the fire inside begin to build and grow. It had been so long, and he was very good. She felt his hands then start to move. First, slowly he ran them down her back and over the curve of her hip, pulling her even closer to him. She felt his mouth slowly leave her lips and trail down her neck and he nipped her collarbone. He moved his hands up her hips and his mouth found her again. The kiss was passionate and full of promise. She felt his hand slip under her shirt and she panicked, pushing him away.

Braden stood frozen, what the hell was wrong with him. He planned on sweet talking... maybe steal a kiss, but this... He ran his hand through his hair and walked to the deck to calm himself. One thing was for sure. She wanted him just as badly as he wanted her, she couldn't deny that now. He looked over at her, she was stone-faced and looked almost sad. He frowned, that was not what he expected to happen, but why would it make her sad?

"Chloe, I'm sorry." I didn't mean to get so carried away." She looked down and then back up at him, a smile now sitting on her face.

"I understand. Like you said, you haven't been home in months. I'm sure you're just tired." She moved to walk back to the door leading to the house. She whispered to herself "Plus it's dark out here, I'm sure that helps."

"Helps with what?" He was beside her, he was like a cat the way he moved.

"Nothing sorry, just rambling as always. I should get to bed, I have to be at work early." She smiled at him, but he knew something was wrong here.

"Sure, I understand." He turned to go and then spun back to look at her. "I like kissing you, Chloe. I won't lie about it, and in fact, I want much more than that. I wanted you to know I plan on trying to make sure you know that regularly." He walked down the front steps whistling. She stayed there until she heard his door shut. She leaned her back against the door to try and calm her racing heart.

The days went by quickly, they would often pass each other in the front yards or as they came home. Both of them caught up in work. He consistently asked her to come over for dinner, but she always had reason to say no. He never made any other move to kiss her or otherwise, and she relaxed more around him. They spent two different afternoons sitting out front talking about life, where each time she was sure they had an audience at all times. One afternoon she opened up more than she planned.

"So, Charlie?" Braden asked as Charlie was throwing a ball with a friend in the parking lot.

"My parents were killed in an accident, he was with them, but survived. That was almost two years ago now." She watched Charlie playing. "He is a good boy though."

"That has to be hard on you, suddenly having a 12-year-old." Braden watched the expressions changing on her face.

"It took some adjusting, for all of us." She took a sip of water from her glass.

"Why aren't you married?" He asked it very matter-of-factly, but with a deeper tone to his voice. She turned to look at him.

"I almost was once, actually."

He sat up at her admission. So, she had loved someone, being close to them. "You know you have to tell me now Chloe?"

"No, I don't Braden." She stood up, brushing off her skirt as she did and headed into her house. He stood and followed.

She noticed him standing in the doorway. "Really Braden, following me into my own home? Even for you that's a bit much." She started folding the towels on the table in the kitchen. He didn't say anything, but methodically started helping. She paused to look at him and he simply grinned at her. She rolled her eyes.

When they were done, he finally spoke. "Why don't you want to talk about it?"

She put her right hand on her hip. "Because it doesn't matter Braden, that's why." As she turned to go he grabbed her forearm and pulled her to him.

"It does matter Chloe, it certainly is part of why you are the way you are."

"What the hell does that mean "the way I am"?" She felt the sting then. She was different. Why did people always feel the need to point it out to her?

"Wait a minute Chloe what do you think I am talking about here?" He took another step closer, never letting go of her arm.

"Let me go Braden." Her eyes glittered dangerously.

"Not until you tell me."

"Fine." She yanked her arm free. "I was engaged, he seemed to accept me." She gave him a glance. "He was always sweet and kind and then when my parents died, he never made it to the funeral. He apologized, and I was stupid enough to believe him. When Charlie moved in, he tried to force me to send him away to a boarding school of some kind.

He said this was not the future he planned and that Charlie was not his problem. So, I refused, and he slept with my friend. I caught them in my friend's house. The worst part was, it had been going on for a long time. She was one of those model-thin blondes. I should have known better." She looked over at him finally and he was in shock. He moved towards her again and she stepped back.

"I'm sorry that happened to you Chloe, he was an ass."

"Thanks."

Her voice was clipped and short now. He knew she was reliving it and it was his fault. He looked at her, she was sad and hurting and it had left something scarred in her. He felt that same feeling when he was put in that home. Like no one understood him or cared to. He didn't want that for her, for her to feel that way. He reached out and grabbed her again and pulled her to him. They stayed that way for a long time, just standing close with him pressed against her until Charlie came running in breaking the spell.

"Chloe, look what I found, a frog!" He happily made his way over to her and she shrieked backing up.

Charlie glanced at Braden, rolling his eyes. "Girls." Braden couldn't help but laugh at the scene before him.

"Well, I have to get going, Chloe. I expect to finish this conversation later." He ruffled his hand in Charlie's hair. "You be nice to your sister." He gave him a smile and he headed out. He had a tremendous amount of paperwork to sort through at his place.

The next week went by uneventfully. She would glance at his place when she went to work, subconsciously hoping to see him. He was a good friend of Charlie, and that was all. School would be out in two days. Finally, it was Saturday, and Charlie was leaving. She knew the Bakers were picking him up at 11 and she started helping him to move his things outside as they waited. He was smiling at her and she finally asked him why.

"You are going to have a whole lot of time to spend with your new boyfriend next door when I am gone, Sis." He started laughing. She swatted at him.

"Charlie, that's not funny. Keep your voice down. He is not my boyfriend, he is our neighbor."

"Okay, so why is he always asking you out?" He looked up at her and started to laugh again.

"I don't know. Maybe he feels sorry for me because my little brother has such a big mouth." She pushed him as she made her way down the stairs.

"No, he likes you Chloe, I like girls at school... that's how he looks at you." He shrugged at her glare and went back to moving things.

"No, he doesn't, guys like him don't like girls... well like me. That's just the way the world is. It's up to younger guys like you to make the world better." She threw a pillow at him and he scrambled to catch it before it hit the ground. Finally, they

noticed the Bakers coming up the side street, and after some
time, he was loaded and leaving.

She waved at him, feeling a little sad at the prospect of
spending so much time alone. Once it had been easy to fill
her time, and now, she was like a mom, and without him, she
wasn't sure what to do. She turned around and Braden was
there watching her. She gave him a wave and headed back to
her house.

He watched her go. It was the longest week of his life and all
he wanted to do was touch her. Between issues with the races,
complaints from other drivers about a leak, and his manager
trying to set him up on random surprise dates at dinner time,
he just wanted something normal. He wanted her. He heard
what she said and it made sense to him now. "Guys like him
and girls like her." She had no idea what he wanted, but he was
going to tell her. He took long strides to her door and rang the
bell. He felt the anticipation curling up. When she opened the
door, he practically fell through it.

"Braden hello..." He cut her off, pulling her to him and
covering her mouth with his. He bruised her lips with his
attack and she felt her defenses slip away. She thought of
nothing but him for a week.

They moved together in the living room and she leaned back
on the couch as he pushed her down. She felt the length of
him against her and it was perfect. His hands were everywhere
and as he unbuttoned her shirt he felt her freeze.

"Look at me Chloe. I want you, all of you just as you are.
Stop fighting me." She was still frozen and he knew he had to

convince her. He pinned both of her arms above her head with his left arm as he moved his right hand over her curves. She was rounded and smooth, and he loved it. She was aware of every nerve ending in her body, as his hands reached around and under each breast, lifting her bra slightly so that the nipples were exposed. He cupped each globe lovingly until he reached the pert nipple that had hardened under his touch. He pulled and tugged on them, creating a deep ache deep down, soon covering each one in succession with his mouth.

Chloe was lost in the sensation. No one had ever taken time with her like this, ever. His hands were lighting her on fire with every movement.

She was all fire, just like he knew she would be. He was almost in pain with the need to rip off her clothes and bury himself inside her, but he wanted to go slow, wanted it to be good for her too. She was laid out on the couch, her hair, a red flaming swirl around her head and yet he could still tell she was nervous. He moved lower to make a final step in making her his.

Her eyes flew open as she felt him slide his hand under her and lift her off the bed as he loved her with his mouth. She couldn't move, couldn't do anything but feel the way he felt against her. She felt the tension fade away and the mounting pleasure begin to spiral out of control. Her legs were shaking as she climbed that ultimate peak to release. She let go of her resolve and fears and put her hands in his hair and let go.

He felt her release, and the way her legs were trembling made him ache for her more. He moved above her and watched her face as he moved to push inside her. She was tight, and it took more than one pushed to fully envelope himself within her. With a final push, he was exactly where he needed to be. He pushed her knees up and over his shoulders as his movements became more frantic, more demanding. Soon, he stood back from her, one hand holding each knee as he pounded into her relentlessly. He heard her moans, and knew she was sharing in the intensity. Her hips moved with his, and the explosion was powerful as he pushed into her one last time and release came.

They both lay there, trying to breathe and trying to make sense of what just happened. For Chloe, it was unlike anything she ever experienced. She looked up at him and he was smiling down at her. He leaned in and kissed her lightly before he stood up. She once again marveled at his chiseled body. He saw her glance and smiled at her. Hopefully she knew that he found her sexy and he enjoyed touching her. He made his way to the kitchen and Chloe quickly redressed. What had she done? She felt the blush rising up her face. He had seen her, all of her. No one ever had. She made her way into the bathroom and then followed him in the kitchen.

His phone rang and she turned to look at him and he frowned as he listened.

"Chloe, I have to go. I'm sorry, something came up."

"Sure, it's fine go ahead." She felt the same fear from before, he would leave now.

"Chloe look at me." She did. "I will be back, I promise. "He kissed her quickly on the head and left.

To say he was worried was an understatement. The 20-minute drive took him 12. He pulled into his lot and stared up at the flaming mess.

His penthouse was on fire and all he could do was watch. He found the house staff and was happy they were okay. The three of them watched as the fire department did their best.

The next few days Braden spent sifting through what had once been his home. His home hadn't been saved and very little else had either. He had to meet with the investigator today and then the adjuster. The police assumed this was an accident, but he wasn't as sure. He was staying at a nearby hotel, trying to hold it all together, but barely. He made sure the staff had rooms and that they were well taken care of. Most of his time was spent on the phone or on conference to various media networks and the racing team. He thought about Chloe, her smile and her sweetness. He missed her. Everything he put into proving he liked her the way she was vanished the night he left, and hadn't come back. He promised, and now she would never trust him again.

Chloe knew she was a fool. She spent that entire night waiting for him, as if she believed in his story, or that he would come back. She waited, and the joke was on her. Life had, inevitably gone back to normal. As a teacher, she threw herself back into the work of planning for the next school year. She found that by journaling a lot, she was able to keep her heart from hurting too much.

The reality was she cared about Braden and what he thought of her. The times they spent talking was a big part of that. He was a kind and sweet guy, despite his obvious fetish for big girls. It wasn't that he never came back that night. The fact was he had never come back at all, until yesterday. She hadn't actually seen him, just that his lights were on and music was playing inside. How he could just ignore her now was the brunt of the pain.

She wished for a moment that she had the strength to march over there and demand an answer, but it was better off left alone. She glanced at the clock and headed out to go grocery shopping. As she did, she heard the door open next door and she cringed. The last thing she wanted was a run in. She turned around and it was a woman, a very thin, very hot blonde woman. The blonde in question gave her a wave and she straightened her shoulders and left.

Braden had cancelled the rest of the afternoon and made the decision to try. He had to explain, and most importantly, he had to tell her the truth. He drove to her place and waited. He saw her car, he knew she was there, but for the first time since he was a child, he was scared. He was a nationally known bike racer and had been with more than a few women all over the world and this one woman had him questioning everything about himself. He felt the guilt like a punch in the stomach. Not just for leaving her like that, but for not telling her the truth about who he was. He finally got out of the car and went to the door.

She heard the knock and frantically made her way to the door. She found a solution to her financial woes and was moving in a roommate. To say the mess from what had once been storage was everywhere, would be putting it mildly. She climbed over the final boxes and pulled the door open. There he stood.

"What do you want Braden, I am really busy." She hoped the nonchalant way she talked to him would fool him.

"We need to talk Chloe, really talk." He sounded serious and she finally made eye contact. Still gorgeous, he looked rough. He looked tired and she knew something was wrong. She moved out of the way and he came inside.

He felt a sense of panic at the mess. "Are you moving?" He glanced around.

"No, I found a roommate. Nice guy, good job." She crossed her arms in front of her and waited. She would let him speak, but she wouldn't make it easy for him.

Braden felt a rush of anger. He would be damned if some "guy" was moving in here. "There are some things I need to tell you and explain. I need to know you will let me explain it all and then we will talk about this "guy" you think is moving in here."

He made his way to the living room and she followed. Her arms were crossed again and her eyes were flashing fire. Even now, he wanted her.

He turned the channel to ESPN and turned to look at her. "This is the best way I know how to explain."

She sat there stunned watching sports news, which she didn't even know existed. Some bike racer had a house that burned down and, wow, he was local. She suddenly felt sick. He was everywhere, pictures and stories and she knew. He turned it off.

"Oh my God Braden, are you ok?" She looked at him and touched his hand.

"I'm fine, my house is gone though. That's where I have been. That's why I didn't call."

"Why didn't you tell me you were famous? It would have made our fling that much more memorable for me." She gave him a half smile.

"Stop it Chloe, I don't look at you like that and I know you don't either. It's more than that and you damn well know it." She moved off the couch and towards the door. He caught her hand as she went by, standing up in the process. He kissed her forcefully, only letting go when they needed air. It was then he noticed her tears. He kissed her eyelids and wiped them away.

"Don't cry Chloe, please, I'm so sorry for everything." He pulled her into his arms and buried his head in her hair.

He kissed her face and then her mouth again. It started so simply, wanting to comfort each other, and soon they were lost in the moment. She pulled away from him and went up the stairs, and he followed. Once there, he took the lead, grabbing her hand and pulling her with him into the room. Their actions frantic now, they undressed each other. He turned her around to face away from him. She felt him unzip her dress and trail his fingers down her spine as the dress slipped to the floor. He reached around to cup her breasts, which overflowed in his hands. He pulled her back against him and she felt the hardness there.

"Don't ever question what you do to me Chloe, feel what you do."

She did just that, taking him into her hand and feeling the length of him. He pushed her over towards the bed and she climbed into it and he stopped her. She was half on and half off the bed when he moved behind her. He filled her suddenly and quickly, and she gasped at his entry. He moved his hand up to her hair, winding his fist in it and bracing himself as he plunged into her faster, and deeper. They moved together both seeking and searching for something. She was the first to reach her peak and she moaned out his name as she did so pushing him over the edge as well. He pulled her to him spooning behind her. She was his, and she always will be. Suddenly she stood.

"You should go Braden." She pulled her dress over her head and stood. He stood as well and she was once again reminded of how perfect he was.

"Chloe please."

"Braden this.... this was a mistake. You know it as well as I do."

"No, it's not a mistake, how can you even say that after what just happened?"

"We come from different worlds, Braden, you're... famous for God's sake and I am just some.." she trailed off. "You lied to me, Braden."

"I know, at first I just wanted you. I was driven by a need to be inside you, loving you. Then things changed."

"No, they didn't Braden... ....you should go... now."

He saw the firm set of her jaw and knew she was serious. He took one last look at her before he left. Chloe waited until she heard the front door shut and she locked it before crumbling to the floor and gave over to the tears.

Braden was not himself. His driving was awful and he couldn't connect with the course. He normally would love the flowing hills of Virginia, but he was officially not on a streak anymore. He angrily threw his helmet into the seat of the car and made his way to the crew. They all knew to avoid him when he was like this. Braden angry was a rare thing, but it usually had a quick turnaround. This time he was like this all day. He was angry, and worried. Chloe refused to respond to any messages he sent her and he missed her. She was so damn stubborn and it hurt that she didn't feel the same way.

Braden made his way into the hotel and caught a glimpse of himself in the mirror. He was dirty from the race, but he was changed now. He spent his entire adult life alone until this one woman came into it and now he was worried about someone else. He knew she had been struggling, in more ways than one. She shared her situation with him, told him her secrets, and he lied to her. He knew she was hurting, but couldn't she see how he felt? He frowned. How did he feel exactly? He got into the shower to wash away everything from the long day. He had to do something, and soon.

He met up with Mike for dinner that evening who put it all in perspective for him.

"You're in love with that chubby girl back home aren't you?"
Braden stood and towered over him.

"Don't ever say that about her again, do you understand me?"
"Whoa, whoa buddy calm down. I didn't mean anything negative about it. I am just telling you man, you got it bad. The whole damn crew is afraid of you the way you're tearing things up all the time. Not to mention you lost your streak, you need to see her and make it right. Either let her go or marry the girl."

Braden sat back in his chair and thought about what he said. Marry her? The thought gave him a start of panic, but the idea of coming home to her, all the time was one he could love. He ran his hand through his hair. He hoped she and Charlie were okay, if only she would answer his damn calls. He suddenly had an idea, one that might make her call him after all. He pitched his idea to Mike, who chuckled and started to make the call.

Chloe was frustrated. The roommate was an ass and he left his things all over her house. More importantly, he was indifferent to Charlie. Treating him like a bug in his way all of the time. Last night was the final straw. He came home drunk and groped her, and she was finished with it. She took a deep breath before knocking on his door. She had to do it repeatedly before he finally yelled something and stumbled to open it.

"What Chloe?" He moaned as she pushed the door open wider.

"You have to move, Josh. I can't have this kind of environment for Charlie."

"You can't just kick me out, Chloe. I have rights. Besides, you like it when I touch you, don't even try to lie." He took a step towards her and grabbed her again. This time she pushed at him and scratched his face. He gave her one blow to the face and she staggered backwards. She rushed to the living room calling for Charlie and the two of them made their way out to her car.

Mrs. Anderson watched the little car pull away with a shake of her head. That was a bad man in there, she saw her holding her face when they left. She pulled out her phone to call Mikey and tell him the plan couldn't work now. After Mike hung up the phone, it took him a minute to turn around. He knew once he told Braden, he would lose it. There was nothing he could do but to tell him.

"Well, what did she say?" Braden was eager to hear Chloe was ok.

"Seems like she is gone man, I mean she had a couple bags and she and Charlie left."

"What the hell do you mean they left?"

"Sit down man I'll tell you everything."

Braden did, only because he knew he wouldn't get any information otherwise.

Twenty minutes later, Braden called the airline and booked a flight to Texas. The sonofabitch was going to pay and he would be the one to do it. Mike tagged along, mainly because he didn't want Braden to end up in jail. They took the direct flight and Braden was full of tension and ready to fight the entire time. Finally, on the ground, they picked up a rental car and made their way into the city. He was practically out of the car before it even stopped. He made his way to her house and when the door opened, he let the first punch fly.

Mike glanced down at the man on the floor. The guy didn't even have a chance. Braden knocked him out with two hits. Braden made his way upstairs and checked to make sure she had yet to come back. He wasn't sure where she would go, she had a few friends, but no one she spoke about enough to give him any clear direction to head in. He walked back over to Mike's and sat in the chair by the window so he could watch and wait. He glanced up at Mike.

"Give me your phone."

"Why?"

"Just trust me, I'll give it right back."

He took the phone from Mike and sent a text to her from his number. He visibly relaxed when he got a response. It was wrong, but it had to work. She would be furious, but he would at least get to look at her and make sure she was ok.

Chloe was concerned. The message said that she needed to come home right away. She wasn't even sure who sent her the message, but she had to find out what was going on. She dropped Charlie off at a friend's house and made her way home quickly. She had so much to figure out and she was exhausted. She glanced at herself in the mirror. It had only been a number of hours, but her right eye was purple and bruised.

She couldn't go back in there. He was horrible. What had ever possessed her to let him move in in the first place? Money, always money. She wanted to keep Charlie in one place with his friends, something she never had, and this is what happened. She pulled into her parking lot and got out of the car. She would wait out here. She couldn't go in there alone ever again. It was then that the door next door opened and she saw him.

It was only a couple of months, but he was perfect. He took a few long strides to get to her and before she could say a word, he wrapped himself around her and picked her up. He literally picked her up. She heard him whisper her name and she closed her eyes against the emotional overflow she felt inside her. Why was he here? She pulled away and he stood back looking her over. When he looked at her face, he swore.

"That asshole." He started walking towards her place and she went after him.

"Braden, wait." She went behind him and they made it to the door. She grabbed his arm. Suddenly there was another man there. He pulled Braden away.

"Calm down man." Braden turned towards her as the police pulled up out front.

"Oh no, Braden the police?" She walked towards the car again. She felt his hand on her arm.

"Yes, the police Chloe. Look at your face and what he did to you." She tentatively touched her face with her fingertips. She saw the rage fill his face again and she touched him. "I'm fine Braden, really."

He watched her go speak to the police and he glanced at the front door as it slowly opened. Josh came staggering out and Mike once again grabbed Braden by the arm, preventing him from going to jail. The police made their way over to Josh and cuffed him. After they were gone, Braden turned to face her.

"We need to talk Chloe, now." He went inside and she soon followed, but not before Chloe saw the blond from before walking hand in hand with Mike. So, she was never with Braden. Somehow that helped to make her feel a little better. At a wave from the two of them, she made her way inside where Braden was waiting.

"Braden, nothing has changed. I love that you came here to help me, I do, but we are still so different. Everything we do is..." She stopped as he kissed her. She closed her eyes, even if they couldn't be together, she could enjoy the way it felt when he kissed her, even just for another moment. She relaxed in his arms and he felt it. He pulled her even closer to him and ran his hands over her curves.

She was everything, and he wanted all of her. The kiss intensified and he undid the back of her dress pulling it to the floor. She was lost in him, his touch and felt the coolness of the air against her skin. She trusted him unlike she had ever trusted anyone else. He pulled her into the living room never stopping the kisses he trailed down her neck. When they made it there, she stopped him. She could be herself with him, for the moment. She walked around him and shed the rest of her clothes. She walked to the couch and laid back on it, fully unclothed and waiting. He watched her, his mouth hungry to touch her, but reveling in the way she was with him now.

She was no longer concerned about if he was attracted to her, or if he wanted her. She believed in him and how much he wanted to touch her. He finally moved towards her, gently moving his mouth down her chest, stopping to kiss and run his tongue over each crested peak. He buried his face in her breasts pulling on them and kissing every inch of them. She had her hands in his hair now pulling his head back up to kiss her deeply. He moved his hands along her curves and she arched up to meet them.

She moaned at the sensation and was aching for him with a need deep down. This is how he wanted her, how he needed her to be with him. He moved his fingers over her, working to a fevered state and he watched the expression on her face as she became more demanding of release. He wanted to give her more and he slid down, burying his face in her and tasting her.

He felt her hands in his hair as she grinded into him and finally he felt her reach that ultimate peak and he knew it was time. He raised above her, his excitement evident and she stood to touch him. Sliding her hands down his body over his chest and further until with a swift intake of breath, she held him in her hands. She slid to the floor, and when he saw her look up at him, it was almost too much. He pulled her up to him and kissed her deeply before pushing her to the couch again.

He mounted her swiftly, pushing into her depths. He reached the full hilt of himself and stopped. He wanted to just feel her surrounding him like this. He looked up at her face. She was flushed from her climax and eager for more, but he wanted to watch the expressions as he moved her. He moved slowly now stretching her to her limits and testing himself, his ability to prolong the inevitable.

He felt her hands on his chest as he looked down at her and he watched her curvy body move with his. He wanted her, always. He pulled out and slammed back into with a force that shook them both to the core. It had never been this good, this satisfying. The need was far too great and they both were aching to reach that final release. He moved faster now, steadily grinding into her and she was almost whimpering, and calling for him. He loved her like this, with abandon.

He increased his speed and was both grinding and pounding into her at the same time. It was good, too good. She called his name as her body moved on its own. She was no longer in charge of it and she felt the orgasm start low until it shuddered through her entire body, leaving her spent and breathless. Her explosion rocked him to the core and he couldn't hold back any longer. He slid his hands under her and lifted her off the bed slightly as he plunged into her again and again until he shared in her release. He buried himself inside her as far as he could. He wanted her to know he had given it all to her.

They lay there holding on to each other. Both afraid to speak, afraid to break the beauty of what they had shared. He knew she would run from him now, but he wouldn't let her. He was in love with her and he couldn't imagine life without her in it. She was the first to move, raising her head to look at him.

"Braden." She whispered and he gently kissed her lips. He held her that way, the two looking at each other waiting for the other to say something else. She was what he had been missing his entire life, she was family.

She raised up, suddenly self-conscious of her nakedness. He knew the person she was in the throes of passion was not who she was every day. It was a part of her she shared with only him, and he loved her all the more for it. He pulled her dress from the floor and helped her into it. He noticed she relaxed some and glanced at him sheepishly as she did it.

"Chloe, before you say anything, I need you to know something." He moved the strands of hair that had fallen into her face as she moved. She waited and looked up at him.

"I am in love with you." I know you don't know how this will work, but I know you have feelings for me too. I know you worry about everything, from yourself, to Charlie and money, and this house."

"Braden" she started, but he held up a hand to her...

"I'm not finished. The last few months have been the worst kind of hell for me. I found my mother dead on my living room floor when I was twelve, and aside from a loving couple who gave me a family for three years, I have been alone my whole life. I didn't even know what I was missing until you and Charlie. I love you. Chloe. I want you with me... you and Charlie. I have more money than I can ever spend and I want to share everything with you."

"Braden... I love you too." He relaxed with her words and pulled her closer to him. She was worried about life with Braden, what she never considered was how awful life would be without him. She smiled up at him and asked.

"Will you miss all the models and thin girls? Can I really satisfy you, Braden?

> "Chloe, what we have is better than anything I have ever done in my whole life. You are sexy and gorgeous, and ALL I want is you." She smiled and a giggle escaped.

> "What's so funny?"

> "Charlie said you liked me even before any of this. Now I have to tell him he was right."

"I love you, Chloe."
He kissed her again, and for the first time in her life, she believed it.

******

About the Author

J.L. Ryan is a bestselling author who has written over 50 books, including the wildly popular Billionaire Boys Club, Billionaire Games, Billionaire Bachelors, and Adventures In Romance. Ryan has also attended numerous book signings and writer's conventions including Romance Writers Of America Conferences. Living in New York, J.L. enjoys spending time with family and friends, volunteering at a large metropolitan homeless shelter, and working in the dog rescue community.

www.ingramcontent.com/pod-product-compliance
Lightning Source LLC
Chambersburg PA
CBHW020918180626
46816CB00007BA/2470